PALM BEACH COUNTY
LIBRARY SYSTEM
3650 Summit Boulevard
West Palm Beach. FL 33406-4198

Dear Parent:

Psst . . . you're looking at the Super Secret Weapon of Reading. It's called comics.

STEP INTO READING® COMIC READERS are a perfect step in learning to read. They provide visual cues to the meaning of words and helpfully break out short pieces of dialogue into speech balloons.

Here are some terms commonly associated with comics:
PANEL: A section of a comic with a box drawn around it.
CAPTION: Narration that helps set the scene.
SPEECH BALLOON: A bubble containing dialogue.
GUTTER: The space between panels.

Tips for reading comics with your child:

- Have your child read the speech balloons while you read the captions.
- Ask your child: What is a character feeling? How can you tell?
- Have your child draw a comic showing what happens after the book is finished.

STEP INTO READING® COMIC READERS are designed to engage and to provide an empowering reading experience. They are also fun. The best-kept secret of comics is that they create lifelong readers. **And that will make you the real hero of the story!**

Jenn — *M. Holm*

Jennifer L. Holm and Matthew Holm
Co-creators of the Babymouse and Squish series

For Kasper

RHUS30394

All rights reserved. Published in the United States by Random House Children's Books, a division
of Random House LLC, 1745 Broadway, New York, NY 10019, and in Canada by Random House
of Canada Limited, Toronto, Penguin Random House Companies.

Step into Reading, Random House, and the Random House colophon are registered trademarks
of Random House LLC.

Visit us on the Web!
StepIntoReading.com
randomhouse.com/kids
dckids.kidswb.com

Educators and librarians, for a variety of teaching tools, visit us at RHTeachersLibrarians.com

ISBN 978-0-385-37403-3 (trade) – ISBN 978-0-385-37404-0 (lib. bdg.) –
ISBN 978-0-385-37405-7 (ebook)
Printed in the United States of America
10 9 8 7 6 5 4 3 2 1

STEP INTO READING®

STEP 2

DC★SUPER FRIENDS™

A COMIC READER

REPTILE RUMBLE!

By Billy Wrecks

Illustrated by Erik Doescher

Random House 🏠 New York

It is a stormy night in Gotham City.

5

The next day, a bank car is robbed.

Batman and Robin
look for clues.

7

Reports of reptile robberies
come in from all across Gotham City.

The Batboat roars into the sewer.

Cyborg and Hawkman follow.

Batman checks the Batcomputer.

It's the bad guy called Croc!

Croc's crew of creatures surprises the Super Friends!

The reptiles attack the Super Friends.
It's a reptile rumble!

Hawkman flips the turtle on its back.

Cyborg seals the alligator's jaws closed.

Robin charms the snake.

Batman lassos Croc.

The chameleons distract the heroes.

Croc escapes in his airboat.

Batman follows Croc in the Batboat.

He chases Croc through the sewer.

Croc leads Batman into the swamp.

The Batboat gets bogged down.

Croc turns his airboat around.

He charges at Batman!

Croc crashes into a stump!

Without Croc to command them,
the reptiles return to the swamp.

31